I Love Y[...]
Dino-[...]

Mark [...]

Illustrated b[...]

BLOOMSBURY
CHILDREN'S BOOKS
LONDON OXFORD NEW YORK NEW DELHI SYDNEY

There's someone here at home
who's lots of dino-fun.

And you'd never EVER swap him
for another dino-one . . .

He's really rather useful
for lots of dino-things.

Like blowing up balloons

And tying them on strings!

The park would
NEVER be such fun
without him standing by.

No one can spin
you faster —

Weeee!!

or swing you
quite so high . . .

And though he has a list of jobs
he has to dino-do,

he always seems to find the time
to play a game . . .

or two!

He's a dino-tastic builder, watch him drive that dino-crane.

He can build the tallest towers . . .

CRASH!

and stack them up again.

And even when he takes a nap,

he joins in with
the fun . . .

he's your dino Sleeping Beauty . . .

He can turn into a monster
and cause a
FRIGHTFUL scene!

ARGG!

Quick, run, HE'S DINO-DEADLY . . .

Yes, he's a
rough-and-tumble dino,

he's the
play-mat-wrestling-king.

He can be your circus pony
clip-clopping round the ring.

He can wow you with his magic –

For G and H ~ MS

For Ian... a Dino-Daddy dude xxx ~ SL

BLOOMSBURY CHILDREN'S BOOKS
Bloomsbury Publishing Plc
50 Bedford Square, London, WC1B 3DP, UK

BLOOMSBURY, BLOOMSBURY CHILDREN'S BOOKS and the Diana logo are trademarks of Bloomsbury Publishing Plc

First published in Great Britain 2015 by Bloomsbury Publishing Plc
This edition published in Great Britain 2018 by Bloomsbury Publishing Plc

Text copyright © Mark Sperring, 2015
Illustrations copyright © Sam Lloyd, 2015

Mark Sperring has asserted his right under the Copyright, Designs and Patents Act, 1988, to be identified as Author of this work
Sam Lloyd has asserted her right under the Copyright, Designs and Patents Act, 1988, to be identified as Illustrator of this work

A catalogue record for this book is available from the British Library

ISBN: HB: 978-1-4088-9344-9

2 4 6 8 10 9 7 5 3 1 (hardback)

Printed and bound in China by Leo Paper Products, Heshan, Guangdong

All papers used by Bloomsbury Publishing Plc are natural, recyclable products from wood grown in well managed forests. The manufacturing
processes conform to the environmental regulations of the country of origin

To find out more about our authors and books visit www.bloomsbury.com and sign up for our newsletters